Harvest Time
at Sheldon's Blueberry Farm

by Melissa Jones

To Daniel,
It's Harvest
Time!!
Melissa Jones

BOOK 3 IN THE BLUEBERRY BOY SERIES

MBP
Melissa's Book
Publishing, LLC

The Blueberry Boy Series
Harvest Time at Sheldon's Blueberry Farm

Copyright © 2013 by Melissa Jones

Published by:

Melissa's Book Publishing, LLC
113 Lynn Street
Harrington Park, NJ 07640

For more information about Melissa or her publication,
visit her online at: **www.writemelissa.com**

Illustrations by Mike Motz

Cover and Interior Design by Daniel Middleton
www.scribefreelance.com

ISBN: 978-0-615-84955-3

Printed in the United States of America

Harvest Time

at Sheldon's
Blueberry Farm

"Yes, Berry Squad, the blueberries are ripe! It's officially harvest time," Sheldon Bilberry said as he walked down a row of blueberry bushes.

He bent and looked at one of the beautiful bushes he had watched grow all these spring months.

He eagerly picked his first berry. He held it gently between two fingers with anticipation, and his eyes started to roll as if he were hypnotized. He lifted the berry and dropped it into his mouth. Blueberry juice excited his taste buds, and for each two berries he picked from the ripened bushes, only one made the basket. His friends, the Berry Squad, watched in wonder, as Sheldon worked his way down the row faster than seemed humanly possible.

The farm in Buron Park was going to
provide Jaloonsville's marketplaces with
their own direct source of blueberries,
freshly picked by Sheldon Bilberry and
his friends.

"Grab a basket, Lou, Neil, Ronnie! It's time we eat. I mean, it's time we pick these fully ripened blueberries for all of Jaloonsville," Sheldon said with a juice-stained smile. "Mr. G, the grocer, and some of the other market owners will be coming up to the farm to get their blueberries."

The Berry Squad and Sheldon formed a circle and put their hands in the center, one on top of the other. "One, two, three …. Blueberries release the power in me! Go-o-o-o-od energy!"

"Dance to the superbness of it …. Sweet!" Sheldon added, and his friends looked at him and laughed.

As the hours passed, the blueberries were picked and the filled baskets started to pile up.

"This is a dream," Sheldon said as he lay, happy but tired, between two rows of blueberry bushes. "An absolute blueberry dream. I am certainly in blueberry heaven!" His mind started to drift. Visions of his antioxidant intake reaching an astronomical level filled his thoughts. And what super powers could he ultimately discover in himself? Sheldon had already rescued the Jalooners by starting his farm. He knew it was only a matter of time before they would need him again.

"Sheldon! Hey Sheldon!" Lou shouted.

"Yes!" Sheldon popped up, startled. "Oops, I was daydreaming," he said.

"The delivery trucks are here to take their blueberries back to Jaloonsville's markets!" Ronnie said.

"Oh ... okay." Sheldon got up quickly. "Hi, Mr. G! Here's the first picking from my blueberry farm," he said proudly.

"Oh, Sheldon! I'm ready to fill up my store with blueberries from the antioxidant super hero!" Mr. G said.

Sheldon and his Berry Squad then decided it was time they opened up the farm to everyone else who was waiting at the entrance.

"Welcome, everyone!" Sheldon said. He and the squad greeted people as they entered the farm to pick their fresh blueberries.

Sheldon's opening day was looking like a success, and everyone from Jaloonsville was there to support him. He decided to give a speech and grabbed his purple microphone.

"I see all my fellow Jalooners took the drive up to Buron Park to celebrate harvest time. Our tiny plants have now grown to bear fruit. The ultimate fruit, the blueberry, Jalooners! *THE BLUEEEBERRRRY!* Tasty, delicious, plentiful, always there for you, what we stand for, what we honor— "

"Sheldon!" Neil nudged him.

"Okay, Jalooners. Go pick your blueberries!" Sheldon said.

Sheldon had just climbed onto his tractor when he heard an unbearable sound: the squishing of a blueberry.

"Berry Squad, I've got some serious business to take care of!" Sheldon shouted.

He drove the tractor around the barn, over the hill, and through the open field passing the side of a pond, and there they were—squished blueberries scattered along a crushed row.

"Stomp ... stomp ... stomp!" Sheldon followed the sound of footsteps through the blueberry rows. "You're breaking my heart. This has to stop!" Sheldon shouted.

The footprints were big, the stomps were loud, and all that Sheldon could ask himself was, who was this person and why would anyone squish blueberries?

The stomper was weaving in and out of the blueberry bushes. Sheldon's feet pulsed with a surprising burst of energy. Leaping over one bush to the next, he chased the stomper through the maze of blueberry bushes. He was closing in when the sound of squishing abruptly stopped.

Sheldon peeked through the blueberry bush and found himself staring right into the face of a big, brown, blueberry-eating grizzly bear.

They both jumped back, startled.

The grizzly bear smiled innocently and nodded—Yes!

"You can certainly eat the blueberries. Just don't drop any and stomp on them! The sound of squished blueberries hurts my ears. And here's a basket for you to put the blueberries in so you don't make a mess!" Sheldon said.

Nodding in agreement, the bear began to pick more blueberries off the bush, quickly filling up his basket!

TODAYS HOMEWORK

When Mrs. Bilberry said, "Story time is over," the kids still wanted to know more about the blueberry boy's adventures.

"Does the bear end up staying on the blueberry farm?" one child asked.

"Do they share their love for blueberries?" another wanted to know.

"Well, Sheldon did see the bear again. He knew that the blueberries kept the bear calm and happy, and he planted an entire section for him to visit and eat." Mrs. Bilberry turned to the door and motioned for her son to enter the classroom.

Sheldon came in and said to the kids, "Sheldon's Blueberry Farm is for every blueberry lover! Look, there's the grizzly bear carrying a big basketful!" The children looked through the classroom windows just as the bear turned and gave them a wide blueberry smile.

CPSIA information can be obtained
at www.ICGtesting.com
Printed in the USA
BVIC02n1447200813
328753BV00006BA

9 780615 849553